opening of new

1ᵗ august

CAPUT XI

K

in dorſa Cetorum

tant anchi

Ich ſtolpert
Irrgarten
-erniß. Etw
über mir. F
oder gefluge
griff m̄ ʒueh
waren die
des Teufel
Schloß, ſe
weiß nicht
dieſem ſchreck
Platz und bin
ʒuruckgekehr

ſchere Caſſe
voon le Go
Lelebure
Milu

For my brother, Stephen.

10 9 8 7 6 5 4 3 2 1

Published in 2006 by Lark Books, A Division of
Sterling Publishing Co., Inc.
387 Park Avenue South, New York, N.Y. 10016

Copyright © text and illustrations Judith Rossell 2002
First publishing in Australia by ABC Books for the Australian Broadcasting
Corporation, GPO Box 9994, Sydney, NSW 2001.

Distributed in Canada by Sterling Publishing,
c/o Canadian Manda Group, 165 Dufferin Street
Toronto, Ontario, Canada M6K 3H6

If you have questions or comments about this book, please contact:
Lark Books
67 Broadway
Asheville, NC 28801
(828) 253-0467

Manufactured in China

ISBN 13: 978-1-57990-950-5
ISBN 10: 1-57990-950-7

For information about custom editions, special sales, and premium and
corporate purchases, please contact Sterling Special Sales Department
at 800-805-5489 or specialsales@sterlingpub.com.

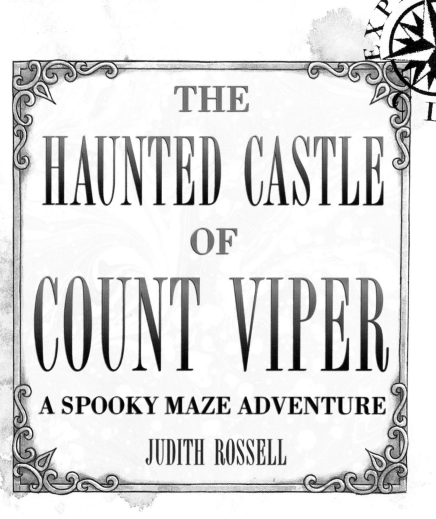

THE
HAUNTED CASTLE
OF
COUNT VIPER

A SPOOKY MAZE ADVENTURE

JUDITH ROSSELL

EXPLORERS' CLUB

LARK BOOKS
A Division of Sterling Publishing Co., Inc.
New York

Madame Racolski,

I have captured your mewling brats. I will return them to you safely when you inform me of the precise location of the Cave of Diamonds.

Doubtless, you will find the relevant maps among your library records. If you do not furnish me with this information, you will suffer the terrible consequences. Your children are locked away and I carry the key with me at all times.

Yours fiendishly,

Count Viper

SCARESTI LIBRARY

The President
Explorers' Club
99 Intrepid St
Valeroso

Dear President,

I need your help urgently! The despicable Count Viper has kidnapped my children, Mika and Elsa. In return for their safety, he demands to know the location of the legendary Cave of Diamonds. I have searched through all the library records and found only one small, mysterious scrap of information about this cave.

Please send one of your members to rescue my children as soon as possible. I am frantic with worry.

I am enclosing a folder of information from the library regarding the many dangers that lurk in the countryside around Scaresti. As well as wolves, poison slugfish, giant cave rats and venomous spiders, some parts are even haunted by ghosts.

To enter Count Viper's castle, you may need to use a secret underground passage. I have found a fragment of a map of the passage, and am enclosing it at the back of this folder.

Please help me!

Yours desperately,

Sanja Racolski

Ms. S. Racolski
Librarian
Scaresti Library

Elsa   Mika   Count Viper

usands of sparkling diamonds tha
idden deep cave of treasure
ferocious, dangerous monste
nt squid that can dro
take care to bri

EXPLORERS' CLUB

Dear Explorer,

This desperate appeal has just arrived from the librarian of the little town of Scaresti. Count Viper has kidnapped her children and is holding them in his castle. In exchange for their lives, he is demanding to know the location of the Cave of Diamonds. The librarian can find only a scrap of information about this legendary cave.

Clearly, your first priority should be to rescue the children but, with luck, you may also discover the whereabouts of the mysterious Cave of Diamonds.

The land around Scaresti is a dark and lawless region, and there are no maps. The countryside is teeming with dangers. You will need to study the notes very carefully. They will help you overcome anything that blocks your path. You will probably need to retrace your steps many times.

Best of luck for a successful expedition!

Lily Leyenda

President
Explorers' Club

P.S. It is believed that the Cave of Diamonds may be guarded by some kind of sea monster or giant squid. The best way to overcome this creature may be to use the famous Medusa Mirror, if you can reconstruct it.

The Medusa Mirror

This ancient treasure has the power to freeze to the spot any person or creature who looks into it. However, in the 1600s it was broken into eight large, gleaming pieces that were scattered widely around the region of Scaresti. If all the pieces are found and stuck back together, the mirror will regain its legendary power.

63

So...

You need to <u>rescue the two children</u> from Count Viper's castle and <u>find the Cave of Diamonds</u>. Use the notes on the folder flaps to overcome any dangers that block your path. You may also need to use the map of the secret underground passage on the back flap. Do not leave the path. Good luck!

Start here

1

8→

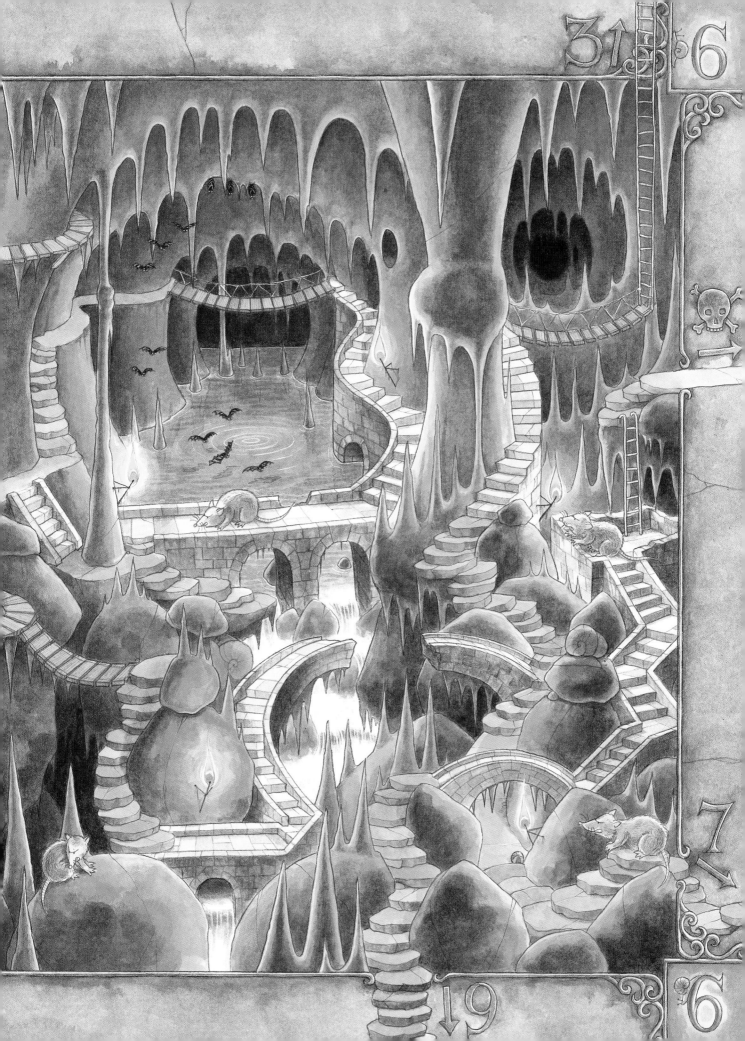

WHICH WAY DID YOU GO?

THE SOLUTION IS ON THE NEXT PAGE, BUT BEFORE YOU LOOK, CAN YOU …

- Retrace your steps through the maze and return to the start at Scaresti?

- Help find Mika and Elsa's toys? They have lost three colored blocks, two balls, a teddy bear, a doll, and a toy rabbit, which are scattered along the maze paths.

- Find the hidden animals on each page? Look at the animals behind the corner numbers to see what is hidden in each maze.

SOLUTION

Secret Underground Passage
(see inside back flap).

Maze 2: Collect Blind
Weed. Walk through
ghosts

Maze 5: Use rubber
boots to walk over
Poison Slugfish.

Maze 1: Collect
rubber boots.

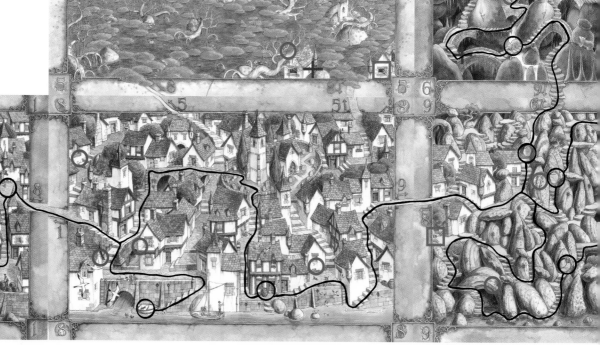

KEY: —— maze path
+ pieces of Medusa Mirror
○ animals behind numbers on maze corners
□ children's toys

Maze 8: Collect torch
and Quik Grip.

Maze 6: Flash torch
to scare away Giant
Cave Rats.

Maze 3: Give Doggy Biscuits to Wolves.

Maze 4: Collect Doggy Biscuits. Overcome Count Viper using Blind Weed. Take key and free children from tower.

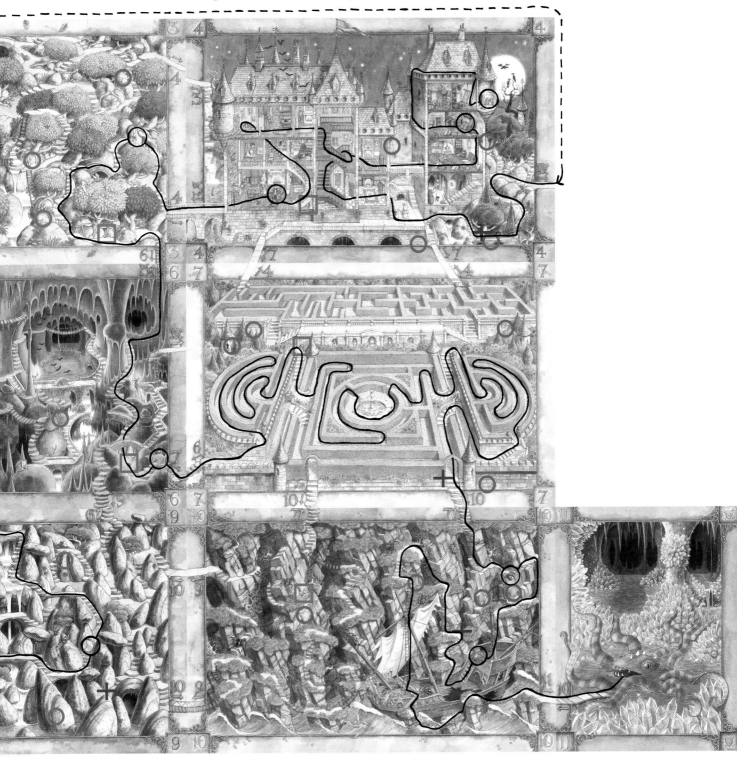

Maze 9: Climb through all four Holey Rocks, to protect against ghosts.

Maze 10: Identify and avoid Venomous Spiders.

Maze 11: Freeze Giant Squid using all eight pieces of Medusa Mirror, glued together with Quik Grip.

In the maze can you also find:

21 BATS

10 CATS

2 GREEN SNAKES

and

13 SNAILS